Mud, Sweat, and Tears

Written By
Brenda Young Montgomery

MUD, SWEAT, AND TEARS

ISBN 978-1-940831-53-4

Published by Mocy Publishing, LLC.

Website: www.mocypublishing.com

Email: info@mocypublishing.com

Phone: (586) 646-8505

TABLE OF CONTENTS

INTRODUCTION

You are about to learn about life on a plantation in Southern Louisiana. Eighty-one years after the Civil War, the experience was a source of healing and reward for a black girl born to a sharecropper's daughter.

One might think this was a pitiful place for someone to grow up, but it was quite the abode. Up until thirteen years old, it was a reality some only read about, heard about, or seen on television.

All the families were sharecroppers working for the plantation owner. This was a regular job that didn't need a college degree. All needed to complete the job was strength to do a day's work. There was no discrimination in the jobs on the plantation. We were all the same. Women had the same chores as the men working in the field. Your family's needs and care still had to be achieved.

We were all normal families caught up in a time of accepting the reality of what we saw in our daily lives. Growing up where everyone is on the same level sometimes saps the motivation for achievement. There was nothing lacking in our needs, we were satisfied knowing that we were safe and secure.

There was a solemn feeling of peace that is difficult to convey. Jealousy and hatred weren't present. Of course, one may wonder, how could that be? Comparing those intangibles to today's society of getting whatever your heart desires, really is a sharp contrast to plantation living.

The plantation life was for each child, a beginning and not an ending. The most important lesson learned was to have compassion and concern for others. This message was promoted by families knowing that each new day would bring about a change. We have to take each day and use it as best we can, knowing that we are in control of our own destiny.

The sharecroppers did their jobs to the best of their abilities. Because of the situations that they had to endure, it didn't interfere with the job they had to do. They would always talk about putting your best effort into whatever task you have. They were very wise; not letting the ideal of slavery put hatred in their hearts.

Everything was associated with the love they had for the Lord, the safety of his protection from the storms of life, and the security they had putting their trust in him. Although, the road ahead seemed difficult, trust in the Lord never would waiver.

As you are reading this book, keep an open mind. The road ahead may not be as hard as you think. Sometimes, we waste time seeking solutions, when the answer is right there.

DEDICATION

To my parents and grandparents, I dedicate this writing. All the lessons about life you instilled in me have been an experience. The struggle you endured for me growing up was a stepping stone to assure a greater life for me. The strength that you displayed in every incident that you encountered was a joy to watch and gave me a sense of security.

Your love for me was always as a shining light. You were with me through my pains when ill and my tears when disappointed. You taught me the respect for others, but most important you taught me about the Lord. Even though you suffered in your life, you still had hope. I thank you for never leaving me alone in time of trouble. You were always proud of me and the accomplishments that I had achieved. There was so much I wanted to do for you. You would always remind me to not spend time on the past dreams of what I wanted out of life, but let life take me to the blueprint of the future that has already been prepared. Also, to remember that time doesn't wait for us, we have to take each new day as an open invitation of opportunity.

Even though you are not here with me physically, your spirit still lives in me. The baby girl that was brought into the world, delivered by a midwife, has grown to accept the challenges that you told me about. Each decision made was given great thought of consequences that may result. Knowing that my future will be only what I decide for myself. I know that you loved the Lord and had faith in his Word. Your legacy will continue through me, displaying a light of love to each person that I meet. I will continue to stand as you did on the Word of God.

You will forever be in my thoughts.

THE BEGINNING

On a plantation lived my grandparents. They were the remnants of families surviving the years of slavery.

Ardoyne Plantation was a rural area housed by sharecroppers. You have read about the shacks and also seen them in movies. It's not a fairytale the shacks were made of dull wood with a tin roof. The outside wasn't a pretty picture. Once inside there was such a breathtaking presence of love that had been put into available material to make the shack a home. Even though the area was considered the quarters, the faith they had that home was what you want it to be in your heart, making it a part of you. It is a fact that everyone can see the outside of an individual and judge on what is seen.

Every house had its own uniqueness. Trees and bushes surrounded the area. As far as you could see were rows of sugar cane moving with the blowing winds. How much energy and hard work had been put into the planting of each row. This was as a city flourishing to be ready for harvest time.

The house had very large rooms. Each room was furnished with whatever they could build themselves. The beds with very comfortable mattresses made you feel as if you could reach the ceiling. The kitchen was filled with wood cabinets and an eating table. The cabinets had a variety of pretty glasses and plates. The wood stove was amazing having a variety of uses. It had racks that were used for baking, which brought about the best in cakes and bread. It also brought heat to help warm the house.

The fireplace was a great source of heat. The heat from it could reach a very large area. It was said that some used the fireplace for cooking their regular meals. It was also a source of baking sweet potatoes and roasting peanuts.

The walls were plain, but still unique. Cutting pictures out of magazines and hanging them on the wall with nails added some class. Sometimes we would use pieces of sticks to make frames. It was amazing how the plantation had the equipment needed to fulfill any idea one could think of.

Grandma wasn't working in the field anymore, but had a busy day with chores taking care of the home. When she worked in the field, I remember her dress code as all the other women. They would have pants on with a dress on top and long sleeves blouses and heads covered with a scarf, hat, or cap. They didn't concern themselves about fashion only earning wages to take care of their families.

Even though women worked in the field, this didn't eliminate their household duties. Having children old enough to assist with chores at home was a blessing. The discipline of each family was the reason they received cooperation. It would mean the family was working together to fulfill each task.

The yard was very large with fencing to keep the hogs in a separate area. The chicken coop had its area and seemed as if they always guarded it. The back yard was filled with clothes lines that saw a lot of use. Washtubs would be used with the famous washboard. Your hands would be itching from scrubbing the clothes so much. There would be a blue rinse to put in the rinse water. Such a different world from where we are in today's society.

Each cropper had land enough near their home to use for gardening. This gave the cropper satisfaction that they were contributing to their family's healthy growth by planting fruits and vegetables. There were flower gardens to make the house pleasant on the outside. The weeds would grow so full and colorful you wouldn't be able to tell the difference. Even though they were pretty the farmers had to separate them from the vegetables or they would be choked and not be able to survive.

There were tractors and plows for digging, but the manual labor was needed for planting and harvesting. Each day was filled with hard work, but the reward was fulfilling. Women and adult children would also work in the fields. Everyone played a part in the development of the family life survival. Arrangements were previously made with the parents and the school authorities. Although the parents needed their children's help, an education was very important.

During the off season the students would make sure they were current in all their classes before the time they would be needed in the field. We see a great change in the generation of today. There are opportunities available, but little interest is shown in taking advantage of achieving and fulfilling their dream.

Once the sugar cane is ready for harvest, every hand is needed. The cane is cut down and put in piles that would be loaded into trucks and delivered to the sugar mill. You could see trucks traveling down the highway back and forth. This would be an all-day activity. The croppers would be excited about what they had accomplished for the owner. This was a life that they had accepted. Not having an education, but able to use reasoning in any task they confronted. They earned their wages and were grateful to be safe and secure with the life they had.

When we hear about the singing and praying of the plantation croppers, it was true it gave them a sense of joy and closeness to each other. The chanting of each person gave them a remembrance of the life each shared. It was a bond that only those involved would understand. The long days of sweat, muddy roads, and nights of tears families had to live through was not easy. Each was living the dream of achieving a life for those who depended upon them. There was a sense of pride and appreciation for what they would be able to provide for their family.

Even though much sweat and pain was endured, they didn't put the blame on anyone. Each took the challenges they faced with inspiration. Wars of men, changes in the weather, and circumstances that occurred didn't make them bitter or take away their determination.

BIRTH OF A DAUGHTER

The farmer and his wife, remnant of a sharecropper's parents were looking forward to the days ahead. Even though they had sons and a daughter, a new birth is about to take place. This was time to discuss the life this child would have to face on the plantation. There always remained the faith in the Lord and hope that everything would be okay. The memory they had of their parent's struggle and the thought of them never giving up during the struggle that they faced. They were always thinking about the families who were not as fortunate to survive. They knew relatives and friends living on the plantation who talked about the struggle that they all faced. But because of their belief in the Lord, who brought their parents through, the same wouldn't let them down.

A daughter was born to an amazing

couple. She was such a beautiful girl, with long black hair. What happy smiles of joy to see such a blessing from the Lord. One would wonder why the Lord would bring another child for them to worry about. They had seen their parents working for the sharecropper to provide for them, now they were in the same situation. The upbringing from their parents poured out the goodness that they should see in all things. They had learned that each situation faced, a solution had already been provided.

It makes you realize what things are important. Most of their lives were filled with work to keep the family alive. The value of family was more important than thinking of themselves. How often do we see this unselfishness around us? It seems that the world is I, me, and mine. It's as if they are looking through a glass, with different characters, seeking only what they can get for themselves.

The baby girl was given a very special name. Now things were about to change from the normal. Making sure the firewood is plentiful to keep the house warm. Mama was taking care of chores and making sure the baby was safe. Papa was working in the field to earn wages for the family. The child grew with loving parents. Not looking at their lives as sorrowful, but that all things are given to us as a test of how we will handle the situation. Having children that are born on a plantation is no different than any born other places. The only difference is delivery by midwife instead of a doctor in a hospital.

As the child grew, there were toys which were homemade. She was amazed at the animals around her. Mom and Dad would sing to her the old spiritual songs they often sung at the community church. The child continued to grow, learning from her parents how good the Lord had been to them. As she got older she began to attend school in the church. School life was not as fortunate as today. As she grew and learned the various aspects of what was taught in class, she began to teach those things to her parents. Knowing that her parents didn't have an education, she felt an obligation to show them how school life can change your outlook. We take for granted all the learning tools we have and don't take advantage of them.

There were quite a few relatives and friends growing up with her. She had many admirers during her school years. Even during those days jealousy was front and center. Young ladies would confront her if they heard of some young man showing her attention. The young men attending school with her thought that she was beautiful and always wanted conversation. She would give them a blush and Papa would make sure they kept their distance. Many would talk about how pretty and bright she was, with such charisma.

There were many admirers of this young lady. Some of the young men thought that they might have a chance with her. However, her heart was for someone else not related to the plantation. Love letters were exchanged to the young man who was in the Army. The plan of achieving goals of the dream she had prayed and talked about with family was the main focus.

All these things she would write in her diary. She had big dreams of overcoming the life of plantation living. Although she didn't degrade this life, her dream was to strive for the greater, not forgetting where it all began. Realizing her parent's life had to have been worst. The faith of God was always in their thoughts. Living in the household of family who had concern for others was a joy. When one hurt we all hurt and there was concern about if the other person can make it. Sharing was the ingredient of everyone that lived on the plantation. The reason being they all worked to receive what they had. No one tried to take from the other.

There was no jealousy of each other. She and the youth of those days dreamed of an education, leaving from the plantation life to achieve their goal. The one thing that wouldn't be forgotten was being able to help the family that they had left behind. The future reached was still possible because of the nurturing the child received in their parent's care. What can we do without nurturing parents? What can we achieve if God is not in the program?

Plantation life showed those on the outside the peace and security that the people felt. Not because of wealth or social status, but the concern for each other and looking for nothing in return. Where else could those characteristics be found, but in the quarters of Ardoyne Plantation.

Attending school was most important to this family. Accepting the great opportunities and excelling in all areas of learning was her key to success. Dreams of her life would be achieved only if motivation and determination was included.   The spiritual guidance from Mom and Dad kept her on the road of obedience and true sincerity.

BONDING LOVE

The wind is blowing, cooling off the heated atmosphere after a rain. My mother and I were having a girlie talk. She felt that I should know some things first hand of my life growing up. We were sitting on the bed of this little plantation house. This wasn't just an ordinary house it was filled with a lot of love. We began to talk about her life and the life she wanted for me. Her dreams were put on hold because she was to bring a child into the world. She spoke of the situation that changed her life. She didn't have any regrets of the years she lived with her family on the farm. The concern was of the disappointment of achieving the dreams she had talked about to her parents. In those days there weren't many choices. The pain she felt for her parents, as she thought of the excitement they showed when she would tell them of her plans of the future.

The road she had dreamed of achieving was as if it was real. Her parents were excited and ready to assist in her plan. Just to see the smile on their face when she would give them the steps that was written from beginning to end. She did the work necessary to begin that road of escape.

The day she had to give the news to her parents of her pregnancy was the worst. It was as if time had stood still. The shame she felt having to give them this news was hurtful. It was as if the world had stood still around her.

She knew that everything now would have to be rearranged. Although her parents were disappointed, their main concern was to support and care for her through this ordeal. She knew that her parents were over comers, living a life that they had no control with patience. Even though they always prayed for something better for her, she wanted much more for them. The main emphasis from her parents was to never let anything hold you back from your dreams. She would always have their support in whatever she decided in her future.

Mother began to tell of this little girl born on a rainy day on Ardoyne Plantation. The midwife took patience with her, being of a young age. The baby didn't give her much pain, but she was afraid. The love of her life and parents were by her side through it all.

There would be a change, but the support given is what brought her through. Having a family who loved the Lord and had the faith, and trust would bring them through. This was a learning that situations occur in our lives to test our belief in God and ourselves. We have to be focused on the journey that is put in our daily living with trust and faith.

Marriage had been talked about for the future, but it became an earlier reality. Life will cause changes to be made, but not be a hinder or block your efforts. There was such a happiness knowing that the baby's father would be with her in raising their daughter. They knew that the dreams they both had could still be accomplished. Loving each other would build the foundation needed to grow and raise a child.

BIRTH OF A GRANDDAUGHTER

One rainy summer night on Ardoyne Plantation, a new birth is about to take place. The grandparents were making preparation for their grandchild. The midwife had already arrived and started getting what she needed prepared. The quarters were quiet, because the families were resting for the next morning work day. The dirt roads in the quarters were muddy and made it hard to maneuver. The rain began to pound harder and so did the pain. It probably was a short time, but it seemed like forever.

On September 4, 1946 a baby girl was born. It was such a relief and blessing that all her limbs were visible. The baby began to cry and everyone was praising God for the blessing. Such a joy that the baby and mom were doing okay. Mom was tired from all the excitement, so she and baby would get some rest. A special name was decided by mom and dad. She said that I was looking like a doll. Everyone came over to see me and wanted to hold me. My dad didn't care about people putting their faces over me, thinking I might catch something. I would be dressed in cute outfits that family and friends had brought over. Most of the items received were handmade and not store bought.

This was a beginning of a new life for the new parents. A young couple with many dreams now had to be put on hold. The love and respect they shared would give them the strength needed to survive the obstacles of life. There would be some disappointments, but a strong bond of love would hold them together. Since dad had gotten out of the Army this would be a different world for him.

As the months passed mother was feeling like a burden had been lifted from her. She could see the growth of her baby girl and the nourishing of family. Such joy and comfort of love she felt. Mama would keep her eyes on me, along with the dog called Mutt. Papa was still working in the field for the plantation owner. He would spoil me when he got home. They would have me on the porch with them.

The dog would always be the guard. The baby was crawling around thinking a lot of ground was being covered. The dog would watch her like a hawk. When the baby would sit on the floor and start scooting he would go and lay down to block her path. That would cause her to turn around and try another way. Thinking back of how young minds start figuring out certain things. They seem to show us that it is not that difficult. Whenever the dog thought she was trying to move from one spot, he would bark. He would be the guard whenever someone would come around the house he would let you know.

The baby started noticing the animals on the farm. Mama and Papa had chickens and hogs. Being able to crawl now, they knew the baby could cover a lot of ground. Therefore, she would not be left alone at all. Starting to grab hold of anything and everything in the way was exciting to her, but not to the dog. You would think he was getting paid for being a baby sitter. I guess his meals and the snacks he would take from the baby was pay.

Now they are really watching the baby every move because she is able to move faster.

Especially when outside and the chickens are passing, she would try to grab their feathers. This was funny, but the rooster didn't think that way.

The dog would be a spy for my grandparents. Sometimes he would pull the girl clothes to keep her from moving. She would get upset with him and try to pull his tail. When Papa and Mama would be planting in the garden, they would sit her down with a stick to keep her busy. They said that she seems to like the taste of dirt. She had to be watched carefully or her face would look like a mud pie. She loved to watch as they planted and tried to do what she saw them do.

The fun would be when my bath water was ready. As you know there was not any bathroom with a sink and tub as we have today. There was the aluminum tubs large enough for bathing. When the tub was filled, the girl would splash and make a big mess. She would sneak the doll in the water with her clothes on. Mother would tell her the doll was clean enough, but it would take a lot to convince her to get out of the tub.

After putting on her warm sleepers she

would get on her knees to pray. After a while the "now I lay me down to sleep" prayer was taught. Afterward she would be tucked in and given a kiss goodnight. She always stated her "not being sleepy" that became the normal statement.

The family didn't have television, but she would listen to the radio. She always wanted to mess with the knobs. She was noticing the different sounds from changing the channels. That didn't work to often if the men were listening to the fights or the baseball games. There would always be yelling, since they would be pulling for different teams. The women would just laugh at them and shake their heads in how they were acting. They would sing songs and was amazed how the girl remembered the words. There was a lot of story reading done by her mother. Pictures of different animals in books shown helped her to identify with the farm animals.

When her parents had time off from their job they would go into town. How excited the girl was to be dressed up. Her father always talked about her walking, and wanting to keep stopping, to look in the windows of the stores in town. This would be something new and different from what is seen on the plantation. She would love to look and smile at the reflection she saw. They would take her to the movies, although she didn't know what it was all about.

The best part of the movie was eating popcorn and other snacks most of all. There would be a lot of bathroom breaks during the show which was a lot of interruptions. She was happy with the common life of family love and security. This was the only life the girl knew and was familiar.

Now she has grown and was able to climb on any and everything. Playing hide and seek was fun pretending that they couldn't see her, but they always knew where she was. Once she was hiding under the bed, but to her surprise there was a bug under it also. Therefore, she didn't wait for them to find her, but called out for them to kill the bug.

In the winter it was amazing to watch the wood burn in the fireplace. She was taught early how hot it was and not to touch or go near the fireplace. She would watch papa put more logs on to keep the house warm. He kept a stack of wood outside to be used for the wood stove and the fireplace. They seemed to have everything ready for whatever the task. The girl would always want to help when seeing someone doing a chore.

Her parents gave her a lot of things to

keep her busy. Family and friends always brought something when they came over. A lot of gifts were made on the farm by hand. There were a few carved wood wagons with special wheels. They would take her riding down the dirt road. She would be bumping up and down, but it was fun. Of course she never wanted them to stop even after being thrown off a few times.

The girl had a big smile when she received a new tricycle. This was great since she was now able to reach the pedal. At first she thought being pushed around was good. After a while that soon changed to the girl pedaling herself to go at the speed she wanted. Even though she didn't want your help, being where she could see you was very important. Even after falling a few times and the bike getting stuck didn't matter. She didn't want to stop riding. One day when riding she saw a neighbor's dog coming, she couldn't pedal fast enough, so she got off the bike and started running. Mutt was chasing the neighbor's dog, but that didn't matter to her.

After attending church with the family, she thought at first this would be a place to walk around like at our home. She soon learned about the Lord's house and the reason we were there. She didn't know that church would be a regular occurrence for her. Attending with the family, clapping and singing like they were, became a learning experience. There were sometimes tears shed at church, she would ask the question, why are you crying? The only answer given was because we are happy. At an early age she realized there was something special about going to the Lord's house. Knowing that there is peace of mind and giving praises for the comfort that it brings to you.

TRUE LOVE

When I think about the life of my grandparents, tears stream down my eyes. Even though I grew up with them on the plantation, a lot of their life they didn't share with me. I suppose it was to keep me focused on the future and not dwell on the past.

Knowing that their parents struggled during their lives was not a hinder to the dreams that they had. Through it all they kept looking for opportunities to come. They trusted in the Lord to deliver them from the trials of life. We have our trials and tribulations and feel that we cannot make it. How would we have handled the life of a slave?

Even though they suffered for many years, that didn't deter them from living each day focused on the belief a change would come.

It was the love they shared with each other that kept them strong. They would laugh, sing, cry, and pray together. They weren't focused on the material things of life, only what was necessary to survive the life they had.

Concern about safety of family was top priority for the sharecroppers.
Each family knew they had each other in time of crisis. They had seen a lot of tragedy and dismay in their lifetime. For this reason they had concern that their family didn't fall into the doom of destruction.

Listening to the stories told to me of other youths growing up with them and their siblings, rebuking the rules of the plantation master were depressing. During those days your strength came from each other, praying and singing spiritual songs. There would always be work for you to do. The sharecroppers continued to have faith that God would answer their prayers. It was important for the churches in the community to fellowship with each other. It was a time to strengthen those who may be weak from the toils of the plantation work.

Even though they always prayed, it was the testimonies that gave encouragement. It goes to show you that we need each other. The most important is to not lose hope. Sometimes there are the circumstances that are out of our control. Supposed my grandparents would have lost hope and faith, what would have happened to my mother?

I wondered about the other youth growing up with me. What they felt about the life they lived. We never really talked about our feelings. Most of the time was spent either in school or helping with chores at home. We also had competitions between each other. We did have friends from other areas, but most of the plantation consisted of family.

Each of us had our dreams of what we wanted out of life. Some married at young ages to get away from the life they had at home. Plantation life didn't come easy for those who let the temptation of materialistic interfere with their dreams. They would sometimes seek after what looks good on the surface and find out it wasn't as it seemed.

FARM ANIMALS

One sunny day all was quiet, the girl was told to sit in the chair and be good. What did that mean? Knowing all the mischief one could think of at this young age. Of course she said okay to being good, but that did not last long. The broom was standing in the corner not bothering anyone, but she decided to do some chores. The broom being taller than her caused a problem. Before she knew it the broom hit the wall nearly missing the light bulb. Grandma came running in to see if she was hurt. The girl was not hurt, but afraid of what was coming next. She put the blame on the broom, but that did not get her out of a spanking.

Now she was given a snack that always worked for a while. She finished the snack, now what's a girl to do? Along came the dog at the door. He is peeping through the screen from outside, and she was peeping at him. She started hitting the screen which caused him to get hit. He didn't like that to good, he starting barking at the girl, so she made barking sounds back at him. The dog stopped barking and started looking strange, as if he was wondering what kind of sound he was hearing.

The girl could hear some young people coming home from school. She would watch until they were out of sight. They would always wave and say hello to her as they passed down the road going home. The dog would always bark as they passed, they would tell him to shut up. This would make the girl laugh and the dog bark even more.

The time is almost here to start kindergarten. The girl was already counting and saying the alphabet, which was exciting to the family. Living on the farm with the animals was amazing, relating them to some of the alphabets, such brightness at such a young age. It seemed everything had something in common. It didn't

take long to grasp what was being taught.

Seeing a butterfly land on the porch seemed to be fascinating, observing their colors. Before grandma could say don't the girl would've started to run thinking she could catch it. Therefore, she learned that they weren't a toy that you could play with.

There was also the fascination of watching the birds calling to them as if she thought they would come to her. One day playing outside the girl saw the neighbor's cat. She didn't have any problem making it come to her. Maybe she thought the cat could be a good pet for her. She thought that after the cat began rubbing against her, making those purring sounds, all was good. After making the cat comfortable, she figured pulling the tail would be fun. The cat did not care for that and began to scratch at her. Therefore, she found out that the cat had to be handled gently. After that experience, when she saw the cat again she tried to hit it with something. It also seemed as if the dog became jealous of the cat. They used to get along with each other, but now it seemed as if they no longer tolerated each other. This was a great learning for the girl that animals have an understanding as people. They think that where they spend most of their time is their property. Grandma and grandpa would always set them straight.

When the parents came home the girl always had a lot to tell of her day. She would try to tell it all so fast, they would have to tell her to slow down. They would be excited that she was making this place home. Learning the surroundings of the living creatures was great living on a plantation, but to her it was home. Wanting always to help with doing the dishes, but they knew it was only to play in the water. She would try to assist in making the beds. The covers would be heavy trying to pull them. They would sure feel good during those cold nights. After being tucked in she could hardly turn over.

There was a string that you would have to pull that turned off the light. The girl always wanted to be the one to do that. When the lights went out it would be very dark, except from the fireplace flame or sometimes a lantern would be on. The family would be singing church songs which would put her to sleep fast. You could see reflections of her colored drawings that had been nailed to the wood walls. All her work would be displayed to show her progress. This showed her parents that the surroundings were not interfering with her learning capabilities.

The mosquitoes were very bad this particular year. They would make a lot of bumps on her which would itch badly. Scratching them would make the bump worst causing sores. Grandma would get the mosquito gun to spray the area in the house. The girl learned quickly that when seeing the mosquito run to get the spray gun. She still wanted to be outside chasing the chickens or watching the hogs. When the hogs would be eating the slop, she would call them nasty and greedy pigs.

Grandma and her chickens got along well. Watching how she cared for them as if they were her children. All the animals knew their purpose and followed the order of things. You could see that they knew who was in charge. It didn't matter if it was grandma or grandpa. The girl tried to pull her weight around with them, but that rooster was mean and would chase her.

The hogs were always inside a fence, so

she did not have to worry about them. They would look at you making those snorting sounds. One day while watching them, one got stuck trying to dig under the fence. He was looking and snorting as if he thought she would get over the fence and help him. She told him that grandpa will come and help you. So he was very happy when grandpa pulled him out.

There was one time she did climb over the fence, when the ball went inside the hog pen area, which was a lesson learned. Just as she was climbing over after getting the ball, her clothes got caught on the fence wire. As she was trying to get loose, all she could see was the hogs coming toward her direction, as if they thought she had slop for their trough. They had a reputation of always wanting to eat.

LITTLE GIRL

Mother and father would buy different books and read to the girl. The coloring books would be a treat. She was taught early about writing on the walls with crayon. Even though the plantation house was made only of regular wood, it was still a home to be proud of. Being read to and relating the things learned to the reality of things she saw was amazing. The things we do when growing up. You are told not to touch, what not to put in your mouth. Thinking back over those times where was the sanitizer? Living on a plantation, no one was sent home for the different allergies, or sickness as today. Was there better attention paid to prevent the spread in school? Even though she wasn't old enough to go to school, she was taught about cleanliness.

Being outside playing with the mud she

didn't want to keep the mud on her. She was always happy to get the mud off her clothes. Mud would get on her mother when she picked her up. She would laugh and say to her, "I got mud on you," she would look at her and smile.

The women in her life were special. The girl was always being taught about being a lady at all times. She would always try to dress herself. Looking back it still goes on. Young girls are still making decisions in what to wear and how to comb their hair. Her mother and grandma had very nice hair. They would let her brush it sometime, until she started twisting as if making curls. When time to get her hair done, it was a different story. Sometimes she would start running, but a snack would win her over.

She loved to drink coffee with grandma and grandpa. They told her later years there would be more milk in her coffee. She didn't care as long as there was a cup for her. Later years when she saw how dark and strong the coffee was, she knew they had pulled one over on her. Now she pulls the same tricks on the little ones today that want coffee. Thinking things over is seeing the love of what family is all about.

Oh how excited the girl was when getting ready for church. She would be singing the hymns that she heard everyone sing. The church members would make her feel good saying how happy they were to have her there to sing. Later years she would be singing in the choir. Grandma and grandpa would be smiling, telling her later that they could hear her voice loud. The people at church would be amazed at her knowing the words to the hymns.

THE GIRL

Putting thoughts back in the past, the talks of childhood was great, the memory of attending kindergarten. Looking forward to seeing everyone dressing up was a joy, wanting to pick your own clothes, not concerned about matching. The little socks with the lace were her favorite. There was a variety of different colors to pick from. The braids in her hair were classy and the ribbons added the extra touch. All the girls probably could've used some perm.

One day at school being upset because her clothes were dirty from playing outside and falling in some mud. They began to tease her, but she told the teacher and they got in trouble. At this point they all got a lesson in caring about each other's feelings. They were all growing up and would be together every day. So they began to be taught about life and growing up. Some of the boys would get into fights. They would start calling each other names. They were a bad group of kids.

Most of the students were relatives and knew the outcome if they acted badly. Parents did not let their child escape from discipline when causing trouble.
There were groups from other plantations that would cause problem. The rumor was because it was said they had some bad parents. So you see those were the kids that would want to take your lunch. Evidently they weren't listening to what they were being taught.

A new life change is about to take place from kindergarten to elementary. We thought, now we are in the big league, Ardoyne Elementary School. It was looking so big and we were smaller than most of the kids there. It was exciting to see the class rooms with seats. So much different from what we had left at the church house.

Being happy and afraid the thought of being with older kids at a new place. This was okay in a way because we still had family there. Now being in a different surrounding was strange. There was a variety of dress fashion, hairstyles, and attitudes. We noticed the change from the little church house to now the school. Growing up into young girls and boys not realizing what future lied ahead for us. Remembering what we all had been taught about what we could achieve in life.

We became anxious to get up in the morning for school. Now is the time you wanted to be neat. Even though not having a different outfit or change of shoes each day, thankful for what was provided. Daily washing of outfits for the next day was a way of life. Most of us didn't have a week wardrobe. We didn't wear all the fancy or name brand clothes and shoes. The most important concentration was an education, which would lead to a brighter future.

We had goals set from seeing our parents and grandparents struggling to provide for us. There were many prayers and tears shed, and being at such a young age, we knew that there were a lot of sacrifices made for us. A lot of us would compete against each other in class. Since she was a great speller, there was always someone wanting to compete against her. The teachers were helpful because they were happy to see smart and enthusiastic students.

Sometimes it was difficult for her when the teacher asked us questions in class. There were young boys in the class that only came to disrupt. When you would try to answer a question they would make funny remarks. Many times she wouldn't raise her hand because of that reason. Then we had young girls who were just as bad, joining in with the disruptive young boys. Thankfully, she had a family that kept her motivated.

The young lady decided she wanted to play the drums. Her thoughts was she would be playing a real set of drums right away. The music teacher informed her that a padded drum had to be made. This wasn't what she had expected. Since living on the plantation where any tool needed could be found, she began the task and the teacher was amazed. After accomplishing what was needed for the class soon she received the drums of her dreams. She received a complete drum set from her family. The family enjoyed seeing her practicing each day after chores. She became a great asset to her class.

When home, she would talk about the young people who after leaving school, had to take care of siblings or chores that would be waiting for them. This reminded her how different their lives were. She was fortunate to not have to work in the field as some had to. Being a perfect attendance holder through all the grade levels was great. This was only due to the insistence of parents wanting to see her accomplish what they could not. Not wanting to miss school was as if she would be missing out on something. She would always want to take something to her friends. After learning how to make popcorn balls, she would take them some.

Being taught at a young age of caring about others, sharing was observed growing up by her parents. So when she would see young people at school being mistreated, it was hard for her to understand. She was surrounded by students wanting to take your lunch or money.

She was teased because of the glasses she wore, being called four eyes, but that did not bother her. The family taught her the important things in life which didn't include worrying about being called names.

One day, while out for recess, her friend was being teased by some young girls. She had real short hair, no fault of her own. She was a very nice person and she didn't want them to mess with her. Sometimes you have to step up in the defense of someone else. To think that they were teasing her about short hair and the generation of today are cutting all their hair off.

How exciting it was going to our new school. The seats at school had a place for your books. There was always someone losing their books and taking another student's. Everyone would put their name in the books, but that did not matter.

One day we had a substitute teacher. The boys of the class were all gentlemen that day. They were on their best behavior, since she was a younger lady than our normal teacher. You would have thought some new boys were in the class. So we girls were just amazed at the change in them. They were answering questions and being helpful. Maybe this was what they needed to hold their interest in school. She was teaching the same lessons our regular teacher taught. I guess the attitude changed because of how she introduced the lesson. She was in our class for a few days and this was an interesting time. Being in the same class each day, you could see the change. It seemed the sub was someone that they could relate to. When the regular teacher returned, she was very proud to announce how great of a report the sub had given of the class. She spoke that sometimes we need a different approach, so that our potential can be revealed. You could see the look on the young boys and young girl faces that used to act up in class. They had such a look of usefulness on their faces. When I went home and was telling the family, it was as if they already knew.

Although we were living on a plantation, some of us had the nurturing of family values. This little school had great teachers and a great principal. They all traveled from town to this little country school. I am sure they could've taken jobs at schools in the city. Remembering how they were all about making sure we all pursued our dreams. Continuing to stay focused on where we want to end up, not focusing on where we came from. Sometimes that would get in the way from our dreams. I spent a lot of time playing games with myself and the animals. Maybe that was what kept me from not concerning myself about where I was. I still relate my life to the little church house where it all started.

MIDDLE SCHOOL

Usually the girl would get home, eat her meal, and go outside to help in the garden. This day was to be different studying for the test tomorrow was her priority of the day. Her eyes were itching so she started rubbing them, which caused them to start watering. Therefore, grandma would put a cool wet towel on them, which always worked. They knew she didn't want to miss school, which would ruin her perfect attendance record.

Now her study time is beginning. There wasn't a television to watch, so there were no distractions. Even though some friends had one, it didn't bother her. She wanted to be the best child a parent would love and support. Her parents would read questions to her, and make sure she knew the answers. This was very helpful because all they wanted was for her to succeed.

Sometimes she would pray to God asking how he let this happen to her grandparents. She told him that her grandparents were God fearing and didn't treat anyone bad. They were always giving someone something that would help their family. Those were the things she thought about. She was a happy child, but sad for her guardian angels. They always went lacking themselves so that she could enjoy better things in life. Grandma would always make sure she had money tied in a handkerchief for snacks at school. Oh how they cared for her well-being.

Grandma began watching as the girl started walking down the road of the quarters beginning the journey to school. Looking at all the plantation shacks as she walked by them. The shacks were as the people of today's generation look at their mansions. It was as though everything accomplished was of value no matter how small. The young men were unable to attend school today, because of having to work in the fields, watched as she passed. Grandma waved to her until she was near the school.

We were entering the classroom to begin our test period. My mind retained the answers from our study form given to us. There was always someone who wanted to see your answer for some question they could not remember. We would give answers to each other on occasion when studying wasn't as important. Those days had changed after growing up and concentrating on our future desires. I remember learning that lesson the hard way.

Not studying for a quiz, thinking it would be easy was a great mistake. When the quiz was passed out the questions seemed foreign to me.

My friend gave me the answer to a question while the teacher wasn't looking. This was a lesson that she never forgot. Although she knew most of the answers, this taught her to always study. There would've been no benefit to her if the answer given would have been wrong. Everyone may have done something silly during their growing up years. Not thinking about all the consequences of being caught. The girl apologized to the teacher for that incident, which wasn't a regular occurrence in her school life. This didn't tarnish the reputation of having a high grade point average or pursuing the important things in life. It was a very special lesson learned of your character which was always taught.

The plantation quarter is usually pitched black at night. There was a rumor that an escaped prisoner may be in our area. The men were all talking about looking out for the families. When darkness set, she remembered not wanting to be near or peep out the window. Every time the dog barked, papa would always have his shotgun ready. He would go out on the porch looking around and the dogs would be right there with him. She would be peeping through the screen door at them. Mama would be rocking in her chair, telling Papa to come into the house. She knew they weren't afraid of anything or anyone. They always taught her to be cautious and aware of your surroundings.

The young relatives would come by to visit with some of their friends. They knew how to carry themselves at our home. Papa and Mama was admired by a lot of them because of their Christian walk and the care they showed to people they came in contact with. Papa was able to communicate with the young men on the plantation. They needed guidance when it came to having a structured life. Mostly they had no idea of future plans except marriage. He would tell them that education would be their only way out. The plantation work had sent them into a different direction in life. He was an example to them, even though they all had fathers of their own. Some women workers lost their self-esteem due to constant work in the homes and field. The children would grow up very fast to be a helper to the mother in the home. Oh how they would have relished the opportunities the youth of today have available.

When passing on the highway, seeing workers in the fields, cutting sugar cane, trucks hauling the cane to the mill, she often wondered how their lives would progress. Some of them never really achieved a new way of life. Maybe since during their childhood, working in the field to help their families make ends meet, took away the desires of achieving any goals, or any dreams that they might have had for their own lives.

The plantation owner didn't disrespect them, but she thinks in some way their self-esteem didn't mature. Although their parents were sharecroppers, this didn't hinder their growth and confidence. They were free, safe, and still able to think for themselves. This way of life was all they knew how to do. As you know, they had no education, but tried to keep the families interested in progressing toward a better way of life. Even though they had to work in the field at times, emphasis was still pushed on the family receiving an education. Spiritually you would find no one lacking.

Ardoyne Plantation was filled with God fearing men and women. What peace we felt walking the roads of the quarters. There was no fear of someone breaking in homes, or bodily harm from anyone. Looking back comparing today's troubles, there was always a sense of concern for our fellow men. It seemed as though we were in another world during that time.

A storm was brewing, the clouds were scary, lightning struck all around you, and it was the sound of rain on the tin roof. Soon the storm would've passed and given us a cool night's breeze. How happy that would be, since the heat of day had reached the high ninety degrees. Even though the heat was miserable, the field workers continued doing their job. Sometimes they would work through their sickness. Not like today, you have sick or personal days. For them no work, you received no pay. This is why the young people had to help their families.

Sometimes there would be trouble between other community's young people, but no one attempted to do bodily harm, only fistfights. Jealousy would be the cause of many feuds. These events wouldn't escalate into dangerous situations or get out of control. Competing against other schools in sports wouldn't cause any serious disturbances over which team won.

On certain occasions there would be school dances, which were considered recreation for the young people. There was respect from students to the teachers. The principal was feared by even the worst student. It was a joy to attend school, although there was teasing, but nothing serious. Sometimes students causing problems were sent to the principal's office for a paddle, even suspended for a few days. All this only helped the student achieve a higher standard of self-control in their relationship with others. This was to teach everyone that school was our second home, the principal and teachers given the same respect we gave our parents.

The girls would wear kang kang slips, starched to make your dress or skirt stick out in a wide circle. We considered being cute with our penny loafer shoes and socks. Oh we were sure enough saying something. As time passed, we grew out of those things because the young men would be looking and smiling. So you see that didn't go over well with the parents. Playing jacks was one of our favorite games. Hopscotch was a pretty good game. We didn't have video games as the youth of today. We were lucky enough to have some families that had televisions. The children of today wouldn't have made it in that situation. The little things back in those days were important like having a fishing pole made from a tree limb, making wagons out of old wood, and finding some wheels to use. Playing hide and seek or catching butterflies. So much is missing in today's society. Therefore we have to hold onto our memories, the one thing no one can take away.

This is what kept her strong and not giving up.

What a joy today knowing that the storm had passed our area again. The roads are so muddy after the rain. It has become a way of life for us. Living on the plantation brings joy and sadness at the same time. Today being Friday means a long weekend ahead. There are usually no big plans as the youth of today. The day would be filled with helping grandparents with chores and playing.

All of us grew up in church. Therefore Saturday was a day of preparation for Sunday church service. We didn't have a variety of outfits, but what we had were used on certain days. We didn't wear our church clothes to school, being taught that church was a special place and should be separated from our daily lives. Young ladies admired their mother and followed in their footsteps in their dress code.

Wearing dresses and hats was a way of life during those days.

Church service was very special. The Deacons would always sing the old spiritual songs, followed by a scripture. Afterwards a Deacon would get on his knees and begin a prayer that would put tears in your eyes. Even though we were young that didn't keep us from having feeling of joy. Being taught about the Lord was a greater way of life for us than our school learning. It was confusing at first, but as the years went by our minds began to learn about the Lord. Learning about the Lord was refreshing. Since we were being taught the bible at home, when the Preacher started his sermon it was as if we were reading along with him. The family would let me read the bible to them daily. This was very special for me, since they couldn't read everything for themselves.

After settling in the classroom, the busy bodies began their usual teasing to anyone they pleased. It didn't bother me or interfere with the plan of the day. Some would talk about what I had on or the ugly glasses that I had to wear. Some would tease about my not having a television at home. These things I wouldn't tell my parents because I knew there were more important things. They didn't know that I was being taught the greater things in life, to know the Lord and be thankful. My family always did everything they could for me. Material things didn't matter to me as it did to others in my age group. I didn't care about having to go to the neighbor house, who was a relative to watch television. When you grow up learning what the value of material things are, compared to meeting the goals that you set for yourself, you shouldn't let anyone deter your direction.

Today we are having a pop quiz. Some of

the students are complaining that we should be able to use our notes. There was always some young man complaining about the work. Usually it is the one who doesn't do anything in class anyway. The teacher would tell them the information has already been covered and they should have some knowledge. This would immediately start a disturbance from them and cause the teacher to put them out of the class. Most of the young people that were sent to the principal's office were repeat offenders. Therefore, it didn't matter to them about being put out.

This school that sat on the highway was special. The principal was a minister, who was concerned about the students. He was aware of many households that had to keep students home, to assist in family needs and to work in the fields. He had a special bond with each student. There had been times when he would take them home on some emergency reasons. He lived in the city, but was quite aware of the life each of us lived on the plantation. I often thought because of him being a minister, God had sent him to us as our guardian angel. Some of the young men would try to provoke him. Due to his knowledge of their family's hardships the student had to endure, caused him to overlook many of their faults. When pain can be seen in someone else's life, how can we turn our backs? Each of us must realize that it could be one of us.

An April night's wind had settled down. Today had been a variety of changes in the season. Usually it is known for April showers, but today we saw rain, snow, and sleet. The winds brought a very cold breeze. People are going to the various errands or jobs. The trees are beginning to bud. The perennials are showing life from the soil. How marvelous is the work of the Lord. We take for granted the revolving of all the things around us. Remembering the days of my youth was as if we knew the next day would come.

One summer day the rain came, the thunder and lightning was very severe. I was sitting, being quiet as I was always taught to do. Mama and Papa always said the thunder was the Lord talking and we would respect that. We would do nothing while the weather was restless. Even the animals would be still. There was a lightning strike, we didn't know what it had hit right then. You could see a pole burning at a distance. The rain pouring down was able to put out the fire, but the wind continued to howl. The house was built with pretty strong planks and we prayed it would stand the test. I was afraid that something was going to happen and it did. Some of the sharecropper's windows blew out of their houses and the tin roof lifted up. The men gathered and provided help where it was needed.

The storm's strong wind seemed to have pulled a tree up from the root in the graveyard. Oh how I hated to pass the graveyard. The trees seemed to always have that moss hanging from it, looking more like a scene from a scary movie. Papa would always tell tales about the graveyard. Many family members are buried there. It is as if you are attending a family reunion when passing by. He would remind me to worry about the living and not the dead.

After the storm passed over, Papa would check on the animals to make sure there was no flooding in the yard and that the chicken coup wasn't damaged. The garden was soaked and they needed it badly. The days had been in the nineties and the ground was dry. For the next few days the weather brought some coolness.

The next day Papa would be checking on the other relatives. Most of them had large families. He found out that some had flooding in their yards. Of course all of the fields were flooded which was good for the crops. They always welcomed the rain after such a long drought. Now everything was back to normal. Mama and Papa said that the Lord had brought the rain to clean what was filthy and water what was dry. He never worried when there was a dry spell he prayed and waited for the Lord to answer. It is amazing how the weather changes in different ways, something that man cannot change.

There were days when they prayed for rain. Some days prayers would be for sunshine to dry the mud that was causing problems with working in the field. Then there would be tears of sadness when working in the heat of the day and having a heat stroke. The plantation was a place of happiness sometimes and a time that you wished you had a different life.

Mama is up fixing breakfast for Papa before he began the daily chores of field work. It is a regular day for the sharecroppers. No matter what the weather Papa would be ready to do a full day of labor. The men on each plantation were always ready. I wondered how this all had begun. It was as if all of Papa's siblings lived on one of the plantations. He came from a large family and they loved each other very much.

The years the sharecroppers spent toiling the fields should have paid off for them. Their devotion to the plantation master should have been a rewarding advancement for them. Even though they were building a nest egg for someone else, no one had their best interest at hand. She sees why the question of today is, where is the 40 acres and a mule? This is why I wonder about all the families whose love ones worked for years and didn't receive an education. Some usually got in trouble because of the life they had lived on the plantation and the choices they made with their lives. This was due to our family taking on the responsibility for the job that they had no control. Their concern began to think what they didn't achieve working those years. Many minds began to regret how their parents were treated and their lives put on hold. Because of their rearing up in Godly homes, they were always respectful of their parents. Papa would encourage the young men to have faith in God. I would pray for us and thank the Lord for the parents that I had. We sometimes feel regret with our lives because of how we feel things should have gone.

She spent many nights with teary eyes. Papa and Mama would be sad sometimes when hearing of death of a relative. They would begin to sing and pray together, and I would join in. There seemed to always be some kind of tragedy. Their main fear was not being able to take care of their family. The plantation life was all that they had. The plantation owner had compassion for the workers and their families. All the workers were treated fairly. This was real and not a fairytale that you would wake up from.

Being one of the young ladies on the plantation that didn't have to work in the fields was a blessing. There were young ladies that weren't that fortunate. Mama was always giving me classes about life as she had given to my mother. She had a lot to say about being a lady. She remembered her wearing hats to church and making sure my head was covered. During the week she would wear a scarf tied around her head. Oh how she loved her aprons that she made from the sack cloths. Everything was so common then, growing up in a family without the outside influences that occurs today. All they cared about was her getting an education. They had nurtured her to be the best citizen possible and to think before acting. Therefore not to let plantation life change who you are and what you become.

It has been a challenge when thinking about what they endured. Some of the things I know for myself and a lot that was told to me. They had a life that was filled with uncertainty, anger, pain, and fear of what lied ahead. But being a Christian, and because of the faith that they had made everything clear about the future. Things started to change, they were getting older. The fieldwork had started to weaken both of them. My mother would worry about them, but they didn't want her to come back there to live. She would travel back and forth making sure all was well with us. I felt bad for my mother whose life had to have been filled with a lot of fear for them. She knew more than I what they really had endured. Therefore I hated to leave them and prayed to God not to take them away from me. Remembering what had been taught at the little church on highway 311 that the race is still on until we are called. Therefore be thankful for the little things. Whenever we would hear of someone's death, fear would come over me of losing one of them. Oh how I prayed that the Lord would keep them safe

Drinking wine was an enjoyment my grandparents had. They let me get a sip, but told me not to get used to it. That wine tasted good to me because it was sweet. The wine gave them relaxation from the memories of past incidents they had seen. Thinking of those who didn't make it through the struggle would put sadness in their heart. They would be talking about different situations that they had faced. The compassion they both had for family was real. Knowing that the dream they had was large, but their hands were limited was heartbreaking. Taking care of them was so much a part of my dreams. I wanted to do so much for them and thought there would be a lot of time to do it.

Taking care of family was a dream desired. Such happiness felt when seeing smiles on their face. They didn't want much out of life for themselves. They only wanted to see the day when their family wouldn't have to struggle. Even though they didn't have an education their counting skills couldn't be beat.

She was in middle school about to graduate, and looking forward to beginning high school. This would mean my leaving to stay in town with her parents. She didn't want to leave Mama and Papa.

Looking back at my early years, they were filled with such amazement. Thinking of the safeness she felt living on the plantation. It was like the vegetable seeds that were planted. She would observe the care Papa took with them after putting them under the dirt, a few days later you could see their heads appear. This was the display of care and nurturing being shown. The tilling of the land while singing seemed to be a relaxation of the wounds that were held within. No one understands the journey that each individual human has endured. Living on the plantation, there was no discrimination. Everyone shared the same workload, same tears, and same joys. It didn't matter who we were, where we came from. The quarter was a community of love. Some may not understand folks that have lived on a plantation. Unless you have witnessed that life, you don't know the road we have traveled. The things that are taking place in our society now weren't heard of during that time. Treating each other as non-human individuals is unbelievable. This gives me the understanding of why the plantation sharecroppers didn't want anything different than what they had known.

We often wondered why we didn't want to leave the place where our family was. Living on the plantation and knowing the difference between then and now, she now understand. Today's society has a category to place each person, according to race, religion, and assets. We are judged on those things and considered on a different level of status quo. The plantation life, they were all considered on the same level. Everyone was standing firm on family values and not family assets.

There were times that the community would come together whether it was sickness, death, or finances, giving and not looking for something in return. The stories we read mentioning slaves that didn't want to leave after slavery ended, those are some of the reasons. We didn't grow up concerned about having or wanting what we saw others had.

The slaves knew that if they couldn't survive, they wouldn't be around the safety net of the plantation. She was told about some of Papa and Mama's family having to endure the treatment of being a slave. What we read about or see in movies aren't made up information. Even though Papa and Mama and the other sharecroppers were free, they still considered themselves the plantation owner's property.

The weather reported a severe storm was in the gulf and growing fast. The trees started blowing very hard and I was afraid. Everyone on the farm talked about if the houses would stand through another storm with heavy winds as we had seen before. We had left school early because of the weather. Some of the students said they were going to do other errands after getting out early, not concerned about the weather. Those were the young women and men who didn't obey the rules of the weather. She knew the danger that often follows when storms approach our area.

Once getting home, Mama had supper already done so we ate. Afterwards she began to do homework which was due the next day if the storm had ceased. Mama started gathering the chickens into the coup, while Papa took care of the hogs. The dog and cat followed their every move. The roads were muddy from the previous rain. The animals were all fed and settled in for a long night. Papa told me that the animals were more obedient to the weather than humans, and she thought about my classmates. They sensed that bad weather was on the way. You could see how they all grouped together and the quietness about them. You would have thought they weren't around.

We listened as the rain began pounding on the tin roof and wind was gusting making that whistling sound. When it started lightning and thundering Mama turned off the radio and I was told to sit still. The winds were so strong you could hear the tree branches breaking off. Water began seeping through the windows therefore Papa started putting rags to soak the water to prevent the water to come into the house. The lightning was very fierce and she kept telling Papa not to get in front of the window, because you could see the strikes. He assured me that he was okay, but for me to be still. We prayed and asked the Lord to protect us and after that Papa said it was in the Lord's hand. No matter what the problem Mama and Papa was my safety nest. She knew everyone loved their parents, but my love for mine cannot be explained with words. The Lord gave us the people in our lives for a reason. It is time that we take heed to the direction that is being given to us.

So we weathered the storm again. There were no major damages, but now the roads were worse than before. The winds began to calm and the thunder was at a distance. The animals were still quiet even though night had not set in. The tree limbs were scattered about along with large branches. Anything that was not secured outside had blown over the area. Some of the neighbor's in the quarter left things out in the elements. Most of the people in the quarters had young children, so a lot of their toys and bikes were left outside. The houses were built on blocks to prevent flooding inside. It was always a good thing for the croppers when it rained, but they were concerned when we got a lot of rain. They just didn't want it to spoil the crops. After the rain stopped, the rainbow appeared. I was always reminded by Mama and Papa that whenever I saw the rainbow it was the Lord reminding us of his promise.

Oh what a great sunny day after the storm had passed. It seemed everything started off full force. The rooster was proving he was king of the yard. He evidently had an attitude about the way the fellow chickens were acting. He began chasing them, but to his surprise a couple of them stood up to him. They weren't going to let him boss them around. She continued to watch as they began pecking at each other, as if they were throwing punches at him. She figured it was best that the young chicks showed him what they could do. She knew that the rooster was bad because he pecked at me many times. Usually I begin to throw something at him and take off running, and Mama would tell me to leave her rooster alone.

It was not enough for the chicks to be in an uproar, now the dog and cat seem to be at it also. The dog had found some food and the cat felt that since they are on friendly terms he would share his findings. Sorry that didn't work out that way. Of course the cat didn't give up that easy. The dog would bark and jump at him, but the cat stood his ground. He was able to reach in and grab a piece of meat and run. The dog figured he would let him go and try to finish the piece he had instead of chasing behind him. The dog had sense enough to be content with what he still had for himself. This showed a lesson that to have something is better than nothing at all.

My day would always be filled with surprises. Now all needed is for the hogs to get out of the pin. Looking in on them, and of course they thought she was bringing them some slop for the trough. They stood looking as if they were waiting for me to do something. While standing, gazing at each other, Papa said they knew it was their normal time of feeding. Pouring the slop into the trough, you could see them pushing each other out of the way. She would call them greedy pigs, but that didn't matter to them. Having animals on the farm is like taking care of your kids. They depend on you for their care and well-being.

While looking at the vegetable garden, she noticed a neighbor's dog digging and having a good time. In a hurry she started to run him away before Papa saw him. Not being any match for him, he began chasing me. Running fast as possible hoping to reach the gate, but he kept coming. All she could say was, feet don't fail me now. By this time Papa was outside and the dog knew his time had come to an end. Papa had a stick, started yelling and shaking it at the dog.

The dog had the nerves to think that he could stand his ground with Papa. He soon found out who was the boss. He gave out a few barks and stumps. Afterwards he left wailing and wagging his tail with his head down with shame. Probably went home to tell his master about the event. This is the usual incidents that you will find on the farm. The animals keep the farmers on their toes. Each sharecropper has a variety of animals. Therefore they experience the same incidents sometime or another. With all of the excitement going on the chickens and cat stopped their bickering and sat down to watch the show. The hogs were full from the slop and all they wanted was to lay in the mud and sleep. It was never a dull moment.

Mama was not feeling well today. Asthma has been a sickness giving her problems for years. I tried to help the best she could when she had this attack. It made me sad and upset because it causes the shortness of breath. She had this powder that she would burn in a saucer to inhale and get relief. Soon she would be feeling better and start on her regular routine. Going to the doctor was out of the question, because they didn't feel secure with them. During those days doctors had a reputation of always wanting to operate. On the plantation if you were sick, home remedies were the medicine often used. After a while Mama began to use an inhaler spray when she felt shortness of breath coming on. As time grew she began to trust the inhaler more after she convinced herself it was good for her. Even though Mama would be sick, she still wanted to continue doing her chores. Mama and Papa were strong in faith and knew God would take care of them.

Living on the plantation was a reality to them. Remembering how their parents had to survive with less than what they had accomplished. Tears streamed down my face whenever I thought about the stories that were told to me about their lives. They had seen their parents live with many pains and sickness. They said no matter what their day had been, hope was never far away. They prayed that their children would have freedom and security most of all. This was a dream that did come true for Mama and Papa. To look back at that time, she realized if they wouldn't have had the faith and hope to believe, and not let anything get in the way, what would have happen to my mother? Would her parents have still been considered slaves and not free. Would the plantation life have been a slavery life for me? She gave thanks to the Lord for making a way for us through all the danger he kept from my guardians. What a feeling of delight she had to look back at those times.

On this cool, sunny day she could hear

the dog barking outside. After going outside, she found him trying to protect the chickens. The rooster was being mean again, but the hen was standing her ground. It looked as if the chicken were trying to team up on the rooster. That rooster had a mean streak he had the attitude of being king of the land. She yelled and waved to him as if that would help. He stopped chasing the chickens and started chasing me. The dog and cat seemed to abandon me, because they knew to stay at a distance. So she started throwing at the rooster and there he went into the chicken coup. Therefore that was the end of his fun for this day, but she knew it wouldn't be for good.

Later that day she told Mama she was going into the chicken coup to check for eggs. Before going in she began to make a security check, since she wasn't the bravest. As she started to survey the area, there the snake was in the corner curled up as if he owned the place. She didn't waste any time yelling and running away. The dog was running behind her barking, not knowing what she was running from. That's how she got the name scary cat. Mama came out of the house and went into the coup and chopped off the snake head as if it was nothing. They are always trying to get the chicken eggs before we could. So this is a normal occurrence on the farm. Mama and Papa weren't afraid of anything that she knew of.

Papa and his relatives would go hunting in the woods across the tracks from the house. They would always bring a rabbit, coon, or squirrel. It would look funny to me seeing the rabbit, thinking about how we eat the chocolate bunny at Easter. They would clean and cook them with sweet potatoes. She would tell Papa not to kill the animals, of course that didn't work. He would always ask if she wanted it for a pet. You know that was a joke, me who would track down a bug to kill it.

There was always a choice of food available. One had to have lived there to really know what it was like. The freedom of having everything you needed right there. Looking at the society we live in today, it is amazing. Being content of the surroundings, when night came everything was quiet. Hearing a dog bark from a distance or our dog barking when he thinks someone is intruding, such peace we felt then. Remembering that the appearance of how your home looked to someone else didn't matter. It was that every house was similar. Once you have a sight on the worldly delights, the mind is blinded about the real purpose. If we aren't careful, we will fall into the trap of the enemy.

The cold winter rain made the roads very

muddy. The only good thing, the cold weather caused the mud to be hard. Therefore, the cars and trucks that would come to visit didn't get stuck. Some of our relatives had very large families, so there was never a dull moment. The younger kids would be making noise trying to take each other toys. This would go on until the parents gave them a spanking. You could see the tears streaming down their faces and the screams as if they really were hurt. We found out later that this was their way of not getting spanked as much. So you see kids were playing games on the parent even years ago.

The grownups would drink and talk loud to one another, each trying to get their word in. This was a joyous time for them to talk about the season and how their crops had done. They would always share with one another, because some crops may not have had a large harvest. Some of the young men would get into trouble because of drinking alcohol and start arguments. There was always the mature one in the bunch to bring it under control.

Young ladies would play jacks on the wood floor being very careful because of splinters. Of course there would always be someone ending up with splinters, which would stop the game for a while. That was a game that I had mastered in my young life. Sometime we would play checkers, but it would be boring. When the ground would be dry, marking the area for hopscotch would be great. Today markings are made on the cement sidewalk.

Young men would be talking about the girls in school and planning to go visit them at their homes. They would be daring each other about if the fathers would let them visit their daughters. They were very polite young men because of the upbringing from their families. It makes you think about this generation of young people. There are very few that shows respect to their elders or men showing respect to women.

You could hear the singing of old spiritual songs when passing some of the homes. They would always give thanks to the Lord for the many blessings received. It was such a joy to know that it didn't take material things to give thanks. The plantation wasn't a place to cause you to lose your joy. It was the beginning of the pathway to what had already been patterned for us.

The girls grew up playing with the dolls and dishes, the boys grew with toy soldiers, cars, and trucks. She began to love the wagon rides. It was always a joy when someone got a bike. There was never a thought about it not being new. It was such a blessing for whatever parents were able to give. The security felt knowing the gift was safe and not having concern of someone taking it away.

It was interesting putting animals and things in the right blank spaces. Putting the states in its right blank on a blank map was learning where they were located. So you see there was always something to learn no matter what the occasion. Most of the parents had no education, but did learn some things from their children attending school.

Things we take for granted now were considered a blessing. Put yourself in the life of a sharecropper and his family. We don't want to share and want everything put on a platter for us. Think of chopping wood for the fireplace, going out to hunt for your family dinner. We want to pick what we eat and drink, and the clothes that we wear. Today's society is caught up in the world of fashion. The less fortunate are teased if they don't dress the same. Many today want to wear only name brand in everything. Does that make you a better person? If so, how did the sharecropper survive through the many years of slavery? It was only because they didn't take anything for granted. They appreciated the works of their hands with the spirit of the Lord being their guide. Using every tool of learning that they had to prepare their family for what lied ahead for them. It takes us back to how important family values are needed.

She was excited about not having to attend school for a few days. My eyes had been giving me problems because they would start itching and begin to tear. Wearing glasses had become a way of life for me. Many days she would awake with eye problems, but that wouldn't make me stay home from school. My parents would try to convince me, but that wouldn't work. I had a reputation to keep up my perfect attendance. Therefore she was happy it was the weekend. A lot of kids would like to stay home and pretend that they were sick. She would always tell them that they should be happy about being able to learn. They would call me a know it all. She would tell them that at least she wanted to know it all. They didn't know it was hard for me. They didn't realize the difficulty their parents had in making a life for them.

It wasn't easy to endure the heat of the day working in the fields. Many days she would pray that the Lord would make it easy for my family. One night while praying that the Lord would continue to protect them and keep them safe, it was as if I could see the future of what I was praying for. Was it a dream? Was she awake and in a trance? Only the Lord knew the answer to those questions. The next morning I asked my family about my dream. They told me that the spirit of the Lord already knew what I was asking before she spoke. At that time it was amazing to me what they said. After being taught more and more about the Lord, I began to see what they meant.

One day the porch planks were loose and walking on them she fell through. Oh what a scary time for her. The splinters were no fun, and being under the porch even for a short time. Not sure when one of those creatures would show up. She forgot about her friend the dog and cat always stays on my heel. They were right there with me looking as if to say, why are you down there? She was rescued from under the house before I became a nervous wreck. Mama and Papa pampered her thinking she was hurt, but thank God she was okay. The old house made of wood and tin was getting worn in some areas. It didn't take long for the relatives to start hammering on the spots that needed repaired. It was always a family affair when something needed to be fixed. All the houses were made the same, some larger than others. There was always something the men had to do. Because of the fear of God in people during that time, love for each other is what kept the bond.

Oh how good the smell of the kitchen on this cold day. Mama had a large pot of soup filled with vegetables from the garden with a soup bone to give it flavor. Everyone who stopped by would be welcomed to enjoy a bowl. The generosity the sharecroppers had whether they had reaped a big or small harvest they would always share. The kindness everyone had during that time was because they had been saved from what could have been a different outcome for their lives. They were known for treating strangers the same as relatives or friends. Knowing we all had something to be thankful, we should never put ourselves as being more important than anyone else.

Thinking of the many times after church, the minister would be invited to come over for a meal. Everyone looked forward to enjoying Mama's good cooking. Sometimes the other lady members would be planning to invite the Pastor first, but it seemed he would always have Mama and Papa on his schedule every time. Perhaps he had become somewhat accustomed to the warmth of their hospitality and fellowship. We don't see much of that in today's society. A lot is missing in the world around us that sometimes we wonder why. There are changes happening all around us that may be hard to put into words. We have to either change with the times or be left behind in the world we remember.

The wind was blowing the trees, which

was changing to such pretty colors. The winter brings a different feeling, changing of the temperature keeping you inside more. The young kids still wanted to be outside playing. We would still walk around outside the school building. We would be talking about current events that are going on in our lives. It was an excitement of seeing each other each day and having a concern of what problems we may be dealing with. We realized how special it was to have friends that were concerned and showed it. To know that what you talked about was only for the people that you trusted.

The winter in the south wasn't as cold as in the north. The rain would make it colder than ordinary. We didn't complain because there was always something to keep you busy. We didn't have access to cars as students of today. If you weren't picked up, you would be walking to your destination.

She would thank the Lord for my guardian angels that made sure my focus would continually be on the Lord being my guide. It would be hard sometimes not knowing what lied ahead. There were many nights of feeling bad for my grandparents who tried to do everything to make me happy it would hurt them when seeing me hurt. Thinking about how my being ashamed to wear shorts because of marks on my legs and thighs of sores from mosquito bites. When coming to the reality that happiness is that you accept who you are as a person.

My friends would be talking about new young men in their lives. We didn't really have what you would consider a special boyfriend. It wasn't that we could go out on dates. We would see our friends only when at school or school events. She was teased about a young man in school, but that didn't develop into anything.

Then she met a young man from another community. He would often send me messages by his relative. This went on for a while. We met each other a few times while attending games at our school. She was really fond of him and felt he was someone special to learn more about. He was quiet, someone that my family would approve of. His family was known by some of my relatives. She decided to make arrangements that he would be introduced to the family.

We found out that we can plan for ourselves, but sometimes it may not be the plan that the Lord has for us. One day after getting to school, it was told to me that the special young man had drowned in one of the ponds in his community. That was a very bad day for me it seemed as if it was all a dream. It showed how life could be taken away so quickly. Therefore instead of being sad about things we have no control, continue to strive for the goal that you set out to reach. We are our own failure thinking negative of situations or problems that may arise. We can achieve whatever our hearts desire if we stay focused.

Some friends decided we would meet and talk about our future plans or desires. We walked along the dirt road lined with sugar cane. They grew so tall you couldn't see someone hiding in the rows. Everyone looked at their life so different. This is the reason you need each other for motivation. As we talked, all of a sudden something made noises in the bushes, we all started running. If this was a marathon, we all would have gotten a medal. By the time we stopped running, we forgot what the conversation was about. So we continued each other giving their points about life.

Someone thought that marrying their

boyfriend would mean being rescued from their large family. They wanted to escape from watching siblings and doing chores, which included cooking. It seemed that spending your life with someone you loved didn't matter to them. Listening to them talk as if to love someone had nothing to do with being committed to that person. Just as the young ladies were thinking about being rescued, the young men were looking for wives to raise a family. This was all that they had seen from their parents. Therefore, it was as if nothing different was meant for them. Plantation life sometimes ended up being an inheritance. All the sharecroppers had been down that road with their parents. On the other hand, they didn't want the same for their families.

Some of us began thinking about graduating from high school and joining the service. We always admired the women in uniform, standing tall and strong. We often talked about independent traveling, not getting married early, and having children was far in the future. There was a friendly relationship with most of the young ladies, but four of us continued through high school. Although, living in different communities, and only saw each other during school days. We played sports together during our middle school years. One of our girl basketball players was very tall and a good shooter. I guess because she could almost reach the goal. Sometimes other competing schools would think she was older. There would be sore losers during some of our games. When their scores were low and time would be running out, they would start playing rough. Our team would let them know that we could play rough also, and showed no fear of them.

Running track was ideal for me. In the evening after school and chores were done, and

Papa had rested from his day, he would time my running speed. Running as fast as I could down the road in the quarters, he would always say, "you are fast as lightning and nobody will be able to beat you." He would still say to pick it up a notch. He would pretend to be a contender. Mama would be looking and telling him to stop me from running like that. Mama was always thinking about me getting hurt. She guessed because climbing the trees was a habit of mine. All was okay until she landed down from one. Luckily nothing was broken, but she still had that memory.

One day practicing my track speed, my ankle was twisted, and Mama was very scared. She started hollering at Papa that she had told him something would happen. Papa wouldn't pay her any mind. They would soak my ankle and put rapping to prevent it from swelling. Once the healing took place, my running continued. I would participate in a lot of relays for our school. We always looked forward to any competition held which gave us a challenge in our field.

What a joy thinking about the days of old, in comparison to the youth of today, spending time with the elders. There is more time spent trying to keep up with what the world wants, has become more of a priority. She believed if each of us would take a step back into the basics of life. We would see what our purpose is meant to be. Stepping back into the shoes of this little plantation girl, who thought there was nothing more pleasant than the life she was living. Today's generation would laugh at the things I thought was a blessing. Not having a week of clothes to wear before washing and not concerned of name brand clothes or shoes. Oh how I wish they could put themselves in a dream that would show them about living such a life.

She realized that this life living with my grandparents was nothing that man had chosen for me. To think about the joy she brought to Mama and Papa was the best that could've happened. This was meant to be a fulfillment their parents had not been able to achieve for them, or what they couldn't accomplish for my mother. Such love and joy that we shared with each other was great. Growing up and being able to use my resources to also help someone else. Learning while growing up to know what was most important in life. Sometimes it may take a while to realize what you have as a child is a jewel. This is something that could not be bought, but can only be received from above. So whatever we think we need, it's not of any importance. How we treat each other is our main purpose in life.

Looking back at those days on the plantation, living all my childhood not knowing how the world looked at this life until later years. The effect of being a different color than the plantation owner didn't matter. This was only due to having a family that taught not to stress about where you came from or how you looked. Only to remember that life will throw a few punches, but we can withstand, if we are true to our belief that we have a purpose. We have to realize that we aren't the only part of the puzzle, but play an important part.

The winter nights were something to remember, the fireplace burning with a low blaze. The wood burned and kept the house very warm. Without the person starting the fire, using their expertise, it would've been a cold house. The covers on the bed would be heavy and well tucked under me, that I could hardly turn over. The women had a joy when sitting around cutting out material pieces to be used for making the quilts that everyone needed for the winter months. We didn't see snow, but the cold was enough.

Most of the boys would be walking the roads at night visiting friends. They didn't need to be afraid as we are today. There were no lights in the quarters, but you could see lights shining in the distance along the main highway. Everyone had their own personal dog that would give warnings each time a visitor came near their home. The young men didn't have stores to visit and just hung around with nothing to do. Respect for others was a way of life that was taught to everyone. We knew that if you did something wrong and someone that knew your family saw you, it would be reported to your family. There wouldn't be any retaliation from the accused. This was the true meaning of needing a village to raise a child.

There was an excitement of going to bed, looking forward to the next day at school. She didn't have to worry about waking up late the rooster was always on duty, although the family would always be up early. Preparation for her day had been made providing clothing and a meal to give strength for the journey.

This little girl lived as a queen in her eyes. Things could've been different for me. The nurturing of love received was more precious than silver or gold. Living on a plantation, but living the same as those in the city. That is why we cannot get caught up in the sight of things. What one sees isn't always the same in the mind of another. Every situation that we face is for a reason. We may sometimes wonder why we are put in them. If we think about taking each situation and handling it in our best strength and mind, we can overcome.

We have decisions to make in this life and it is up to us how we handle them on our own.

During the winter days she would set my chair close to the fireplace. Of course Mama would tell me to pull my chair back. The heat felt so warm and good to my skin. She wasn't realizing the heat was burning the skin, even though it felt so good. Putting sweet potatoes in the fireplace to cook was great. There was always supervision in any task she would tackle.

Helping out with the chores was great, such as washing on the washboard, which was in a tub full of water. There was a blue liquid that would be added to the rinse water. The washboard would make your hand itch after rubbing for so long. We didn't use gloves to protect our hands back then not thinking about keeping the hands soft. Some people might have had gloves during chores, but we didn't. Afterwards we would hang the clothes on the lines in the yard. What a fresh smell when they have dried from the sunshine. Washers and dryers weren't a convenience for our family during that time. Sometimes the storms would threaten, and we would have to hurry and bring the clothes in before the rain started. There are times now that my family hangs clothes out to get the fresh sun smell. It brings a special joy to my heart that some things we don't forget or push out of our minds because of society.

Looking back at the years that has gone by, but the memories wasn't forgotten. It's as if writing about those experiences put me back in time. It is such a blessing from the Lord to give me the memory of sharing with someone else. The tears of joy and regret that enough wasn't done during that time to help achieve more. Everything that occurs is evidence that trials that enter into your life isn't by chance, but a direction which has already been set for you. It's always what steps you may take from that point. My main wish is that during those earlier ages she would've grasped hold of more things that was important. This has always caused me to beat myself, because she didn't take charge of situations in my life better. Not letting the situation become a blockage from what is important, but a lesson that we learn from.

Being a child, there is no concept when losing someone. They are in your life and we think they will always be there. My youth helping plant the vegetables was just doing something. It wasn't looked upon about the end results or benefit that would be received from doing the job. Maybe there was the comfort of someone else looking out for me. Working the garden, singing songs was a relaxation to my grandparents. The little things that we take for granted.

Sitting on the porch in the rocking chair enjoying the cool breeze was great until the mosquitoes run you in. When going into the house, some of them usually get a ride inside with you. There would also be those already inside waiting for you to show up. She would like to spray them with a mosquito gun. Mama or Papa would have to tell me that I had sprayed enough. Sometime she would stand in a chair or even on the bed to kill them. She hated the tune they would sing in your ear when trying to sleep. Yes, living on a plantation, but still a normal life as today.

As long as there is breath in your body we will have decisions to make. Some of my family and friends that grew up and attended school with me are no longer alive. Therefore, she believed the legacy of my youth should be told about such a life. Thanks to the Lord, for good health and the mind to remember the days of old. The roads have been a challenge to follow, but not as the toils that the sharecroppers endured. Putting yourself at the location of the events is very personal. How precious the memories are if you put yourself there.

The cold days are gradually leaving. We looked forward to the new season. The grass starts to grow and leaves begin to gather on the trees. The farmers look forward to growing their crop for the months to come. Even though this would mean the plantation owner's crop would have priority over everything else, this didn't matter to them. She would often wonder, but never asked about the man and his family that lived in the big white house. No one really complained or had any harsh words about them.

The sharecroppers got up early, before the rooster makes his crow. The animals begin to wander around the yard, each in its own world, knowing that daylight has appeared. So wonderful that the animals understand when darkness sets in that it is time to lay quiet. Even though the dog lets them know when there is an intruder, they still make a sound. The trough is filled with slop for the hogs. Corn is shucked for the chickens. All this is the big preparation for the next day's feeding. The dog and cat make sure that they aren't left out.

The tractors and old trucks are making the rounds picking up the workers taking them to the field. Some would walk to the field area they are scheduled for the day. Everyone would have hats and scarves on their heads. The sun could be very hot during the long days. When watching movies and showing the worker's in the field, wearing scarves on the head is real. We sometimes think some things we see is make believe. All of this writing is real life stories.

We as young people looked forward to seeing each other the next day. Funny how we never thought that the next day wouldn't come. All we thought about was having fun at school. After school we would pick fruit from the trees. The blackberries were very sweet and juicy. Picking the fruit was fun, but eating them was the best part. The only thing I was careful about was making sure no crawling creature would be around. It was known by all that she was not brave when it came to the outdoors.

Summertime brings nutrients for the harvest. It was the time when crops would grow and hopefully not get drowned by too much rain. The plantation owner would be looking forward to harvest time as well as the sharecroppers. The bad thing about the rain was the mud. The mules would pull the wagons through the mud. Afterward they would try to shake as much off they could. The men would wash and brush them down. Shoes would look bad and vehicles would get stuck.

The tractors would have to pull quite a few trucks and cars out of the mud. The tractor was a great benefit because of the large tires. The owner and his helpers would ride the horses looking over the area. The workers didn't have any problem dealing with working in the mud. They looked forward to reaping the benefits from all of the hard work they did. What peace and joy they all seemed to have when caring on their daily activities.

Today's society thinks that their jobs are most important. Even though we work for the owner, is it any different now as it was then? We think because we have the material things the world offers, we have achieved and never think we have enough. Because we have built our morals in what our eyes can see, it is all for nothing. The sharecroppers had their eyes fixed only on family values. It didn't concern them about wealth and fame. Treating each other as being important not according to assets or status. This could only have been brought about through initial parenting. Looking back she sees a mirror of greatness. This is only brought about through life looking glass. This glass will only let you see yourself then and now. What do you see? Was it worth the years spent living that life? The regrets will always try to take hold. We have to know and realize it was a path set for us. We have to accept the decisions we made carrying out the plan.

Looking back at the plantation life of a

little black girl, walking the roads of the quarters not aware of what lied ahead. Having no idea what was waiting for me on the road that would be paved for me. Through all the trials that arose brought me to reality. Unless you have a relationship with Jesus, our Savior, nothing will ever fall into the plan that has already been created for us. We look around and see all of God's creations and should be receptive of the fact that no one could have done this, but God. Please don't be deceived in what man tries to put into your mind. Some say that it was a bang that brought all of this to existence. She was glad that her life growing up in the plantation shack opened her heart to the reality that one day she would have to make a choice in her belief. Being reared by a God fearing family, kept me on the road of knowing for myself, nobody, but Jesus could save her.

Walking the roads of the plantation was

something very different from what we see today. Young people are walking with their heads down and phones in their hands. They are innocent to what is going on around them and the traps that awaits them. We cannot blame them if the adults are showing the same example. Nothing will change until we each realize that it is we have to make an impact in this society. Each of us is a looking glass to someone. What they see in you is how they will base your character. It is important to display a positive attitude to all that may see you.

The Christmas holidays are approaching and people are excited. She started to wonder about the occasion. It seemed that they were more concerned about giving gifts to each other than praising the gift already received. Each new day receiving the breath of life is another gift from above. More importantly, Jesus is the gift that will never be replaced. We are so caught up in the view that the world allows our eyes to see, which looks good and brings about the temptation to want it. Our ears begin to hear the things that we feel our soul need. After desiring all of what we have seen and heard, does it make our soul complete?

Oh what a great season to celebrate the birth of our savior. There was strict teaching during those days of being appreciative of whatever the gift. The wish list was simple each child knew their family's situation. Children tearing open gift wraps, having expressions of happiness. The years of my youth living on the plantation during the holiday was very special. We had a good time with the toys we received. They were wrapped in brown paper bags. There were some things in colorful sacks. They celebrated the true meaning of Christmas. The tree was decorated with homemade items. The house was filled with the smell of many dishes. Family and friends stopped by to greet and praise the birth of Jesus.

Such emphasis was made on the blessings that we had received during the year. The family had seen some happiness and pain, but through it all we had survived. What great joy to see my family's faces when opening the gifts they received. It was such a thrill using my talents in creating different gifts. Thinking of today's society that much emphasis is put on things bought and what is spent. We were very happy with the little things. Knowing that your family had to endure sweat and pain to provide the things we received. Working in the field wasn't something that they had picked for themselves

Seeing the big cast iron pot with boiling water, you knew this was a special occasion. A hog would be killed, skinned, and hung. The meat would be cut in a variety of sizes. The intestines would be cleaned and washed several times. After cleaning, they would be cooked with special seasoning. Today we know them as chitterlings. They would be cooked outside because of the smell that would linger if cooked indoors. The pot would also be used to cook crackling which would be the fat cooked in hot oil.

Listening to the various plans for the holiday, do we ever say if it is the will of God? We take for granted that we will see tomorrow as we have each day passed. She has grown to realize that the only thing that I have a guarantee is going to happen is death. We cannot control our destiny, so why not prepare for it. They prepare for family and friend's visits by cooking the various dishes, with activities filled with the joy of fellowship. Even though it was a joyous time greeting and feasting, it was only temporary. The problems and situations faced before haven't gone away. The thought of friends and family so worried about things of the world, seems that they aren't concerned about their soul salvation.

We confess to be Christians, but we continue to do the things of the world. It is not acceptable to say and not do as you say. We are truly who we say we are, when nothing can persuade us, or we don't compromise to be accepted. The growing up years was dear to my heart. Everything we received was given with compassion and was an addition to each child's growth. Today everything is considered a tool that will keep the child busy and on their own, getting them out of the parent's hair. When are we going to stand up for right and not convenience? Only when a tragedy happens, we realize that a different decision should've been made.

Being a Christian is a daily walk, with the mindset of being the best person you can be. This walk requires not letting the flesh overpower your thinking, which is not an easy task. This is why the spirit is constantly fighting with the flesh. Our eyes are tempted when we see something that is of the world. We are tempted over the things we are familiar or already aware of. The enemy knows our desires and our temptation therefore it can be used to his advantage. This is why it is important to train the child while he is young. When you are taught the difference between good and evil, it is a starting point of the growth in an individual. I am proud of my upbringing and hope to continue being a shining light of love, that I am an ambassador for my Savior, Jesus.

THE GREEN STORE

The store located on the highway was an asset to the sharecroppers. Since the farmers did not have money to pay as they shopped, the store allowed the families a credit account. The store was made of wood with a porch. The inside had the hardwood floors that would squeak as you walked. It was well kept and items organized. They carried most items that you would need. They had catalogues that showed a wide variety of household items not kept at the store. Most of the dry goods were sold in cotton sacks. The sacks, being colorful would be made into aprons and some into scarves.

Material would be bought to make some clothing and curtains. The bed linen and some curtains were ordered from the catalog if needed. Some clothing was on hand, but most would be ordered. There were even a large variety of dishes and cooking utensils to choose from. The cast iron pots and skillets were the sharecropper's choice of cookware. Those items are still being used in today's society.

Along with the wood floors, there were pots and pans hanging on the wall. Washtubs and basins filled the corner of the store. The aluminum washtub was used for bathing during those days. There is such a difference comparing the tub of today.

The store being across the street from our school was a plus. We would go over on our lunch period to buy snacks. Yes, there would always be supervision when crossing the street, because the highway was very busy. It was amazing to my friends that I could put what I wanted on my grandparent's account. The owners were very friendly and always knew my name, since I visited there often with my family. Sometimes they would have her snacks ready before she asked.

The store owner and workers showed respect and politeness to the sharecroppers and their families. The store had been vital to the plantation sharecroppers for years. We have to keep in mind that this was a place the sharecropper could always depend on. Most of them did not have transportation. Therefore, this place was in walking distance. They could go to purchase items for their family on credit. The malls and shopping centers are the mainstream of today's society, but we have to pay as we shop.

Visiting the store on several occasions, the building gave a feeling of warmth and safety. Maybe since everyone was familiar with each other. Everyone would greet each other with a smile. You would not see the youth just hanging around. During those days the youth always had chores that took the majority of their time. There was no fear of someone breaking into the store. Today's crime shows that respect for people and property has been lost.

Friends visiting my home always had a good time. There would always be a variety of snacks and cold drinks. Mama would always have a nice meal for anyone that would stop by. They would always praise how good everything tasted. Some of my friends felt that I had it so good. Maybe they all had other siblings living with them, and I was the only child with Mama and Papa. She guessed it was a blessing to not have to share with other siblings. That taught me a lot about sharing with others.

The green store is still standing on highway 311. It still has the same look as previous years, a little facelift in some areas. Instead of selling grocery items as in years past, it has become an antique supplier. It was great to purchase books and other special items. Looking around the store brought back memories of the days of old. The most precious of all was to see a copy of a receipt showing items charged on my grandparent's account. The owner graciously permitted a picture to be taken of the receipt.

It is so special to have memories of those times and not be ashamed to share with others. Unfortunately, I cannot share with loved ones that are no longer with us. This is why it is so important to cherish the challenges that we have endured in our life. Looking back where it started, knowing that it was the step that put me where I am today.

CHRIST BAPTIST CHURCH

A little white wood church located on highway 311. This was a comfort zone for the kindergarten students. Looking forward to seeing your friends and most of them were your family. We had such great times learning, but a better time playing outside. Even though there was a graveyard next door to the church that didn't seem to bother us. I guess because we were taught that the dead weren't who we should be worried about.

Benches were used as desks and also as our tables when eating our lunch. We usually shared our lunches with each other. There were peanut butter sandwiches, fruit, snack, and always milk. Peanut butter is still going strong in this generation. I don't remember anyone being allergic to peanut butter during those days.

Pews were made of wood same as the floors, but was kept clean as possible. We were taught not to treat the church as a place to play. The teacher was very good to us. We would be excited to see her every day. She would tell us about how little girls and boys should act and treat each other. Listening to her was as if our parents were the teacher probably because we would hear the same at home.

The girls would wear mostly pants to school, because of running and falling. Our parents made sure our clothes were clean. The girls would all have the standard braids, sometimes a few ribbons. They were not like the braid styles of today. There would mostly be one in front, each side, and two in the back. We all thought that we were cute. My glasses didn't do me any justice. Mama would always tell me that I was still the prettiest in the class. Even though being called four eyes during my young years, it didn't hinder my accomplishments. Mama and Papa would always tell me not to worry about what people say about you.

This little church became my refuge during kindergarten. Going there during the week and happy for Sunday to wear my pretty dresses, enjoying dressing up like the grownups. Church was considered a place of renewing strength from the week of toiling on the plantation. This was the time to give thanks to the Lord for all the blessings they had received. Singing and praying was uplifting to everyone that attended. I was not baptized as of yet, but clapped and sung with everyone. We only had the piano back in those days.

There were good times at the church, attending school or worship service. We learned the pledge of allegiance at an early age. There was always prayer in school during our school years. Early learning was a plus to the young people on the plantation. It made us aware of the comparison in the world we live. The family was devoted to this little church. They left a memorial of lights across the front of the pulpit area of the church.

Growing up in the church, learning about the Lord was inspiring. I wanted to sing in the choir. Sometimes they would let me sing with them. Then one night I told Mama and Papa that I wanted to get baptized. I would always watch the candidates as they gave their life to Christ. After a time when they felt I was ready, my time had come to be baptized. I would sit on the front row along with the other candidates. There was a revival during the week which was called the examination. Before baptism Sunday, we had to give a testimony of why we wanted to be baptized. When approved by the Pastor it was settled. The baptism was held in the pond across from the church. Now I was considered a member and able to be served communion.

Now on the 1st Sunday we would be dressed in white. There would always be a covering on our head on that Sunday. Women only wore skirts or dresses. No one wore sleeveless at any time. We were taught that church was a sacred place at all times. This was taught at home and carried onto church. There was a very high standard of each individual family. My spiritual growth continued, singing in the choir, participating in many programs.

HOPE LIVES ON

Oh what a day to look back at all the goodness that the Lord has provided for us. Even though, there have been a lot of trials, through it all I have depended on the blessing from the Lord. My impatience didn't get me anything, but disappointment and disastrous trying to do it on my own. What a waste of time and effort to finally realize that the Lord promised to not leave us nor forsake us. I know it is hard to believe because of our human nature. When we look back at where the Lord has brought us from, we can only give praises. People are carrying on their daily activities, not being concerned that this could be their last day here on earth. My parents and grandparents left me with words of encouragement that will always be remembered, to treat each day as if it may be your last. No one knows when, where, or how our life will end. We do know without a doubt, there is an end coming. Making preparation for that day is the best gift of all.

THE ROAD AHEAD

We will never reach our goals in life if our purpose in life hasn't been realized. There have been many of life challenges, but through them all a lesson has been learned. It is all about helping someone else, giving a kind word of hope and encouragement. We are only on this earth to be a servant, not looking to be served or expecting something in return. Even if visiting the sick and shut-ins is the best we can give to someone. Each day there is a change in someone's life. We never know when it will be ours.

There were times in my life that fear had control of me. It was not the fear of losing or getting hurt, but of taking that step and not knowing the end results. Looking back over my life, I never accomplished dreams from childhood of being able to care for parents and grandparents who struggled to pave the way for me. These dreams were desires I had, but knowing now that all of the things dreamed were mine and not the Lord's plan for me. Even though, the Lord's plan for me will not be seen by loved ones that are gone, they will by someone else in need of my service.

Realizing that failures in my life were due to not believing the way had already been paved for me. Now laying aside the focus of my shortcoming and begin to lay the foundation of a new beginning. The time is now to think about life with the spirit of the Lord dwelling in your heart. There is joy that will fulfill your inner soul and give you the strength when you think you cannot make it.

The old dreams now are paving the way for the new direction the spirit has for me. Unlike the dreams of old to please the world, but the new dreams are directions that give hope and love to the lost. We have a purpose beyond what the world offers. When we concentrate on things not achieved is a waste of time, all is vain if it is not to please the Lord.

My focus now is the original purpose on this earth. If you haven't started on that path, you have not opened your eyes to reality. Therefore, you are walking in darkness and may never see His marvelous light. The past years are gone, but the memories of time spent with family are still in my heart. Those years are gone forever, but most important are the years to come.

So the nurturing in my youth was the beginning of the life to come. The background, living on a plantation, was to be a reality of today. Where would I have known about it unless reading about it? To have lived it is a better lesson. How blessed to be able to remember the way it was, all praises to the Lord to have given me parents who loved Him. They didn't look at their circumstances, but kept their mind on the word of the Lord. Realizing they weren't alone in their trials no matter how rough it may have gotten.

Thinking of relatives and classmates who because of their family's needs, had to miss school to work in the fields. This reminds me of how special my life on the plantation really was. I was the fortunate one that didn't have to work at all. What great memories not being ashamed of the way life was. I am very proud of the people that were in my life. Cherishing the teaching received about being a good citizen. Living on a plantation, believing that loving the Lord and through the spiritual tutoring from my parents, He would come to my rescue. We didn't have the best in material things, but the love we shared wouldn't be taken away.

NO REGRETS

Another day to reflect on the time spent with grandparents is as if their presence spiritually is with me. Trusting in the guidance of the Lord in my life is what has kept me. Each new day I get strength to take me on this journey. It is a vague picture, but for some reason I am taking the steps necessary.

If you have never felt that something is missing in your life, or that there is something you should be doing and not doing, concentrate in that area. There have been roads that led me to various places not good for me. My Christian journey in past years was a glass frame with many cracks. During my youth days church was a reality for me. As I grew older it was beginning to be sort of a tradition that was done with no goal thought about. It was something to do on a Sunday or weekly night service. Only until you receive an understanding of what being a Christian is all about you know nothing. Those were the days that are regrets when grandparents and parents were showing the reality of it all, but we weren't enthusiastic to grasp it.

Reflecting on the times of old, thinking it was all about having fun and going places. Looking back it was only the prayers of parents concerned not only of our safety, also asking forgiveness for our wrongdoing. So now it is all about being real, spending time with fellow believers mean something. The days of going along with the majority even when not for righteousness are over. There is a point in your life when soul salvation should mean something. As long as there is breath in your body a change can be made.

So we have to start somewhere. We have to realize that the church is you. Therefore changing churches doesn't do anything for your soul. You are in control of everything that happens in your body (church). We sometimes feel that to change from a certain place instead of seeing the situation change will benefit us. It is all about contributing to the cause for a solution and not being the cause of the problem.

We think our status will reap benefits. I realize what was told to me as a child has all come to reality. Man will be with you if it is for his advantage. Promises will be made and broken. It is only when we see the light of what is real for ourselves.

Each new day should mean more to us than what we gain for ourselves in worldly benefits. Our soul inheritance taught early in life should now be the ladder we climb. I know we expect promotions at work, even at church. Which plaque will guarantee your soul salvation? As I stated, younger years were spent playing church, now it is real not counterfeit.

Oh what great joy remembering the old days. We relish the moment of being able to feel safe and secure. No matter what each day may bring, it is met with comfort and joy. The world of today's generation does not even realize how fortunate they are. We are caught up in things of this world, feeling as if they are of more importance than anything or anyone else.

We wonder about tomorrow and plan ahead for different events. How often do we think about our soul salvation? What will happen when tomorrow comes and you are not around? Do we ever think of those things? The time is now to put a part of you into the reality of life.

Each new day should bring about a

change in our thoughts and deeds. It should never be the same as the day before. Only when we put life's challenges in the right prospective, a change in our daily living will occur.

On earth we find ourselves in a deep valley and cannot climb out. We encounter mountains that we are not able to climb over. We think that we are in this situation alone. Only until we put our trust and faith in our savior Jesus Christ, who can remove any obstacle that may come in our path. Jesus will able you to go around anything that maybe in your path. Put your trust and faith in him, who is able to do all things.

We are our own enemy. Our desires of the flesh will take over if we are not equipped with the power of the Holy Spirit. Put on the whole armor of God to withstand the wiles of the devil. Remember, only what we do for Christ will last.

ENCOURAGEMENT

It is time to put into print what your mind is bringing to your thoughts. Sometimes it is a period of time that we do not have control or aren't aware. It is the thoughts of our past that intrudes our self-control. When we think about it, we are not doing ourselves justice when we let our mind become controlling. We cannot let our past take over our present thoughts. Who we are and who we become is up to us. We have to realize that no one is to blame for our shortcomings or our mistakes.

When this world throws us a curve, we have to be ready and willing to face it head on. The result will not always be what we want, but will mainly fit our need at the time. We have to realize that our need in this world will outweigh the wants and desires that we may feel.

We are our own person and able to take control in any situation that erupts. When we open our eyes to reality, only then will we see the light. Why we do not try? It is because of our fear of failing in this society. How can we fail if we never give it a chance?

Wake up to the world of reality.

CONCLUSION

Readers I thank you for taking the time to
read about the life of a
black girl on a plantation in Louisiana.
This was a stable place dwelled by her
grandparents, working as sharecroppers.

It showed how a family could enjoy the
blueprint that life has drawn out for them
with love and comfort. Working as
sharecroppers, not owning anything, but
still putting every effort to complete
whatever is put before them.

In everything there is a beginning and an
ending. This was where the child was
molded and shaped in becoming a unique
citizen to be proud of. This growth was

the help needed to prepare for what lied ahead in school life on the plantation.

This is only an ending of growth in one stage, making way for the start of a new life with its episodes of high school continuing to pursue the rewards life has to offer.

Isaiah 40:31 - *But they that wait upon the Lord shall renew their strength; they shall mount up with wings as eagles; they shall run, and not be weary; and they shall walk, and not faint.*

Made in United States
Orlando, FL
08 February 2022

14595999R00102